PANDA SCHOOL

adapted by Ellie O'Ryan

Ready-to-Read

Simon Spotlight

New York   London   Toronto   Sydney   New Delhi

SIMON SPOTLIGHT
An imprint of Simon & Schuster Children's Publishing Division
1230 Avenue of the Americas, New York, New York 10020
This Simon Spotlight edition July 2015
Kung Fu Panda Legends of Awesomeness © 2015 Viacom International Inc.
NICKELODEON and all related logos are trademarks of
Viacom International Inc. Based on the feature film "Kung Fu Panda"
© 2008 DreamWorks Animation L.L.C. All Rights Reserved.
SIMON SPOTLIGHT, READY-TO-READ, and colophon are
registered trademarks of Simon & Schuster, Inc.
For information about special discounts for bulk purchases, please contact
Simon & Schuster Special Sales at 1-866-506-1949 or
business@simonandschuster.com.
Manufactured in the United States of America 0615 LAK
2 4 6 8 10 9 7 5 3 1
ISBN 978-1-4814-3707-3 (pbk)
ISBN 978-1-4814-3708-0 (hc)
ISBN 978-1-4814-3709-7 (eBook)

All day, every day,
Po and the Furious Five
trained with Master Shifu.
It was hard work,
even for the Furious Five!

"Master Shifu, we spend hours training every day. Why? We are good enough already," Po said. "Because you are all that stands between the innocent and the evil," Master Shifu replied.

Po thought that the Furious Five had trained enough!
"True warriors must always be at their peak," Master Shifu insisted.

At that moment,
the Croc Bandits struck.
"Puny shopkeeper, tremble in fear!"
Fung growled.
But no one was scared of the
weak Croc Bandits.

The Furious Five burst into the room. "Here is where I beat the Crocs all by myself, using just my pinkies!" Po said. *Wham! Bam! Slam!* In seconds, Po had beaten the Crocs, every single one.

"How awesome was I in there?"
Po bragged. "If anything, I may
have been a bit *too* awesome!"
"Do you think you don't need to
train so much?" Master Shifu asked.
"Fine. Po is in charge of training."

"No way!" Tigress said.
"Yay!" Po cheered.

The Croc Bandits searched for
someone else to rob.
Then Fung spotted Master Jia,
who wore a mysterious mask.
"Hand over your money and you
won't get hurt!" Fung yelled.

"Or you could hand over *your* money and *you* won't get hurt," Master Jia replied.
The Croc Bandits cracked up!

"Then I guess you have nothing
to fear," Master Jia said.
He leaped up, flipped through the
air, and kicked each Croc.
Wham! Wham! Wham! Wham!
Wham!

Then Master Jia offered to teach them how to beat the Furious Five. The Croc Bandits started training right away!

Training with Po was easier
than training with Master Jia.
The Furious Five flew kites,
ate pie, and lounged around.
Life was perfect for Po!

Meanwhile, the Croc Bandits learned strength, discipline, and kung fu.

Soon the Croc Bandits were ready.
They looked for someone to rob.
There was just one problem—
other bandits were there first!

The Croc Bandits used their skills
to beat the bad guys.
They weren't Croc Bandits anymore.
They were Croc Heroes!
And they even got a reward!

When the Furious Five showed up,
Po charged at Fung.
Fung jumped out of the way.
Po landed flat on his face!
"Whoa," Po said. "It looks like
you've been training."

"It looks like you haven't,"
Fung replied.

"Sure we have," Po said.

"How is a pie-eating contest
training?" Tigress demanded.

The Crocs beat the Furious Five.
They were out of shape,
out of practice, and out of luck.
Meanwhile, Master Jia had
a special message from the emperor.

But the Crocs were so busy
being heroes that it took a while
to deliver the message.
Whenever someone needed help,
the Crocs showed up before
the Furious Five.

"I don't understand it!" Po said.
"There is only one master who could
teach them so much so quickly,"
said Master Shifu.
"Those who train with Master Jia
are virtually unbeatable."

"So you're saying that the way to be better than the Crocs is to train really, really hard?" Po asked.

"Exactly," replied Master Shifu.

Then Fung delivered the emperor's important message.

It was bad news.

"The Crocs are the new Furious Five," Master Shifu said.

"Woo-hoo!" Fung cheered.

He had a big plan.

The Crocs would only protect villagers who paid them money.

Soon the Crocs would be rich!

Po grabbed the scroll.
"Maybe it's not too late to fix it,"
he said.
Reading the scroll gave Po an idea.
What if Master Jia trained
them instead of the Crocs?

The Furious Five found
Master Jia in the bamboo forest.
"This will be the most painful
training you have ever experienced,"
he warned them.
"Booyah!" Tigress cheered.

With Master Jia's help,
the Furious Five trained harder
than ever before.

"You have trained well, my pupils,"
Master Jia said.
"Even me?" Po asked.
"Yes, Po. Although perhaps
with a little more crying than
the others," Master Jia said.

Po challenged the Crocs to a battle.
The fighting was ferocious.
But the Furious Five had trained
more. They quickly won!

"I used to think training was something you did until your kung fu was good enough," Po said. "Now I see kung fu *is* training. It's something you have to live. Every day."

Master Jia agreed.
Then he took off his mask.
Master Jia was really Master Shifu!
He had finally taught Po the
importance of training—
just in time for Po to take a nap!